HELP!
MY
BROTHER'S
A
ZOMBIE!

Other books in the Nightmare Club series

A Dog's Breakfast
Guinea Pig Killer
Mirrored

HELP!
MY
BROTHER'S
A
ZOMBIE!

BY

ANNIE GRAVES

Little Island

Help! My Brother's a Zombie!
Published 2011
by Little Island
128 Lower Baggot Street
Dublin 2
Ireland

www.littleisland.ie

ISBN 978-1-908195-15-9

Book design by Fidelma Slattery

Printed in Poland by Drukarnia Skleniarz

Little Island received financial assistance from
The Arts Council (An Chomhairle Ealaíon), Dublin, Ireland.

10 9 8 7 6 5 4 3

*For all my sleepover friends,
except Matthew (who's such a dork)*

Annie Graves is twelve years old, and she has no intention of ever growing up. She is, conveniently, an orphan, and lives at an undisclosed address in the Glasnevin area of Dublin with her pet toad, Much Misunderstood, and a small black kitten, Hugh Shalby Nameless. You needn't think she goes to school — pah! — or has anything as dull as brothers and sisters or hobbies, but let's just say she keeps a large cauldron on the stove.

This is not her first book. She has written four, so far, none of which is her first.

Publisher's note: We did try to take a picture of Annie, but her face just kept fading away. We have sent our camera for investigation, but suspect the worst.

THANK YOU!

People are *so* much less interesting than toads and evil cats, but Deirdre Sullivan is pretty strange for a human being and I would like to thank her for her help with this story.

And I suppose the cryptic Mrs Flitcroft should get a mention, too – she'll know what I mean ...

H

ey, this is
me, Annie.
I'm the one
in charge here.

I mean, look, every
year, it's my house.
My sleepover. My dad
who sprays the fake
cobwebs on the window.
My mum who makes the cake with the
black and orange icing and the jellies on
top that look like worms.

(You thought I didn't have a dad and a
mum, right? I don't. I just made them up
right now. To make me sound more ...
well, normal. But it *is* my house. My
cobwebs. My toad. And my adorable
black kitten. I order the cake from The
Gravediggers, in case you were
wondering.)

Everyone who's sleeping over has to tell a story, see. It has to be a scary story. Because if it isn't scary enough, you're out. That's my scary rule. I get to make at least ONE rule IN MY OWN HOUSE.

If you're out, you have to pretend you're sick. So you ring your mum or dad and get them to come and collect you.

Last year, we sent Matthew home. I mean, his story was *useless*. It was about a ghost that said BOO and waved these *swords* around. What an idiot! Everyone knows ghosts don't say BOO. They say BLEURRRRGHHHHHH. And sometimes they don't say anything at all. They just *attack*.

Anyway, this time, it's Jack's turn. He is going to try and convince us all that his brother (what brother? he hasn't even got one) is a zombie. Yeah, right. Way to go, Jack.

ack looked at us.

He had dark circles under his eyes, as if he did not get much sleep.

'I've never told anybody this before,' he whispered, 'but I have an older brother.'

'Rubbish,' said someone.

Everyone knows Jack is an only child.

'No, really,' said Jack. 'My parents keep him locked in the attic. I think he's a zombie.'

Somebody gave a nervous giggle.

'Look, you're supposed to tell a story, not tell us stupid stuff about your family.'

'I'm telling you,' said Jack, 'his name is Stephen and he's a zombie. Do you want to hear about him or don't you?'

Nobody said anything, so after a short silence, Jack began to speak ...

He was a lot older than me, Stephen, but he never minded taking lots of time to teach me things.

Things like how to choose the best twigs to make a catapult out of.

Or how to give a proper Chinese burn, the kind that hurts for days and days and days.

He made me practise on the kid next door. (That kid deserved it. He was dead mean. We saw him kicking a puppy once.)

Just
after Stephen
started secondary
school, the change began.

When he got home from school, he
didn't have much time to play with me.

And even when he did, he wasn't really
there. His head was somewhere else,
somewhere far away where I wasn't
invited.

He didn't like me any more.

I tried being really nice to him, but that only annoyed him.

He was mean to Mum and Dad as well.

He started staying up late at night, and it was really hard to get him up for school in the mornings.

All he wanted to do was hang out with
his friends. I would see them on the
street together, all thin and shuffly.

Their eyes would be flicking around like
they were looking for a way out.

Only they weren't trapped.

And then there was the smell.

Like socks that someone wore in a football match and then left under a bed for six months.

Like the puddles you find on street corners when there has been no rain.

Then he stopped taking showers. I never liked showers myself. They always seemed like a big waste of time. You have one and then, a day or two later, you have to have another, all over again. It all seemed a bit pointless.

But Stephen stopped showering *completely*.

Mum and Dad tried to make him, but he was too big for them to manage.

Sometimes, flies would land on him, and crawl across his face and clothes.

After a while, he stopped bothering to brush them off.

He looked sick all the time. I said to Mum, 'Stephen's green!'

She told me that Stephen was growing up and that it was all part of being a teenager.

She said the smell was a part of it, too.

Next time we went shopping, we bought him some deodorant.

And we got scented candles for every room in the house.

Mum said that would make things a bit better.

Things didn't get better, though.

They got worse and worse.

Stephen got grumpier and shufflier and smellier until, one night at the dinner table, he tried to take a bite out of my arm.

That was *it*.

When I came back from school the next day, Mum and Dad told me that they had sent Stephen to a boarding school for troubled kids.

They said he needed better care than they could give him here.

But it seemed to me like they were looking for a way out of the room when they were talking to me, and I'm not sure that I ever really believed them.

Things went back to normal for a while.

Then one day I needed to get one of the Christmas decorations from the attic.

It was the star and I needed it for this spaceship I was building in my room.

The attic door used to be a normal, wooden-looking one. But now it was big and made of metal. It had five different types of lock on it.

I asked Dad about it and he said I was not allowed to go near the attic any more.

When someone tells me not to do something, it usually makes me want to do it even more.

That's how it was with the attic door.

I used to sneak up there when I was supposed to be doing my homework.

I would press my ear against the door and fiddle with the locks.

I thought I could hear a draggy, floppy kind of sound every now and then, and once I was almost sure I heard a groan.

But the door was very thick.

I could have been imagining it.

AAANNNN

The next thing was, the pets in our neighbourhood started to go missing.

First, next door's dog disappeared. Then Mrs. George's streetwise cat, Ragamuffin.

Everyone was worried about it, because you couldn't know whose animal would be next.

For once, I was glad Mum and Dad hadn't let me get a dog of my own. I used to ask for a dog every Christmas, but Santa never brought one.

He must have known something about my family that I didn't know.

SQUEAAK!!

BUMP!! ●●

THUD!!

One cold, dark night, I woke up frightened.

I'm too old to creep in beside Mum and Dad like I did when I was little, but that was what I felt like doing.

I kept hearing weird squeaks and thuds – sounds that were not like normal night-time sounds at all.

Like 'bumpbumpbumpbumpTHUD!'

Or 'SQUEEEEEEEEEacckkkkkk'.

I decided to go out and see what the noise-maker was.

If it was something silly, like a radiator, I could go back to sleep.

If it was something like a dinosaur, I could run for my life, but at least I'd know about it. I would not like to be surprised by a dinosaur in my bedroom late at night.

I know that they're extinct and not all of them even ate meat, but still ...

Sometimes when the lights are out and everything is dim and full of creaks, I forget everything from my big bad book of facts and start thinking with another bit of my brain.

Dinosaurs seem possible and so do vampires and demons and cat-eating monsters with claws where their fingernails should be and bright red flickering tongues.

That's the thing about the night-time.

I didn't get very far that night.

You see, when I tried the handle of my bedroom door, it was locked.

I was trapped inside my own room.

I lay on my tummy on the floor and I squinted through the chink between door and carpet.

It's small, but you can sometimes see quite a bit if you squeeze your eyes in just the right way.

I lay there for what seemed like ages, and I think I might have just begun to doze off when Dad's big feet tramped past me in their slippers.

Someone else's feet were there too, in black socks with lots of holes in them.

It looked like Dad was dragging the other person past, because their feet were all limp and pointy, like they were being lifted and pulled at the same time.

There was another 'THUD!' and then I couldn't see anything for ages because something was dropped beside the door.

It smelled of dog-slobber and leather. But of something else as well. Something tinny.

I tried to fit my finger through the chink but it wouldn't squeeze through. I don't know why I didn't shout for someone to please let me out.

Something told me that it wouldn't be a very good idea, I suppose.

After a while, the thing got lifted up,
then Dad's feet went up the stairs,
shuffle, thump.

Then came the sound of locking doors,
and Dad's feet went past the other way.

I went back to my bed, hid under the
duvet and closed my eyes.

In the morning I tried to pretend it was all a dream.

Even when Dad was so tired that his head tilted right down into his cornflakes.

What was going on?

I mean, was my
dad the pet thief?

Or my mum?

Or was it Mr Black
Socks?

And why?

Who *was* Mr Black Socks anyway?

Was it Stephen?

But Dad couldn't drag Stephen.

Stephen was too strong for that.

Way too strong.

Unless he was unconscious or something.
Like, if someone knocked him out.

He was supposed to be away at school
anyway.

Not that I believed a word of it.

I wanted to make sure that my bedroom door wasn't going to be locked from the outside again.

So I filled the keyhole with Play-Doh and hoped for the best.

Dad and Mum didn't notice what I'd done because they were busy nailing all the windows in the attic shut.

Parents are so weird.

I wasn't surprised to hear from Nick the next day at school that his dog had disappeared during the night.

That doggy smell outside my door the night before came back to me.

I tried my best to stay awake that night, but it was hard and I didn't manage it.

In my dreams, I thought I saw a shadowy figure looking at me with eyes that I remembered from a face I used to know.

It was a weird dream, not scary, but it scared me.

Especially when I woke to find a human
fingernail beside me on the pillow.

Did you know our fingernails go right
down into our finger?

They have this bloody root that keeps
them in place and stuff.

The fingernail on my pillow had a bit of
skin attached to it, grey and knobbly
with purply clots of
blood gripping to
the bottom like
full stops at the
end of
someone's life.

I screamed and Mum came running.

When I showed her the fingernail, she said, 'What fingernail?' and put it in her pocket.

I told her that I hadn't been imagining it.

And that I would keep on looking and poking around till she told me the truth, so she might as well get it over with and save us both the trouble.

She let out a big sigh and called my Dad.

They both held my hand and we climbed the attic stairs together, as a family.

We unlocked the door and there was Stephen's bedroom, perfectly recreated in the attic. Except with chains.

There had to be chains, see, to keep Stephen from getting out.

It was *his* fingernail.

I knew because his finger was all bloody
where the nail was missing.

He had dug it into Mum earlier, she said,
when she gave him his dinner.
It must have fallen on my pillow when
she went in to check on me. She took it
out of her pocket and
showed it to me
again.

It was still
disgusting.

Stephen always gets a little bit excited around dinner time.

That's because he is kept cooped up in the attic with nothing much to do.

Mum and Dad can't let him out any more, you see, because it would be dangerous.

People would be afraid of Stephen.

They wouldn't see past the green face, the flaky skin, the patchy looking hair. The smell.

The long curved nails and yellow teeth.

The eyes with red in the white bits.

The growling.

But we see past all that because we are
his family.

We have to love him and take care of
him because he is ours and nobody
else will.

He is our little secret.

And if he likes to eat a dog or a cat or a rabbit, fur and bones and all, every now and then, isn't that a small price to pay?

I mean, why shouldn't we give him food when he's hungry?

The sort of food he likes and deserves.

Live food.

Our Stephen has changed but he's still
my brother.

Brothers have to look out for each other.

Even if that means that Dad and I have to sneak out after dark once or twice a week and drive to a neighbourhood where the dogs are free to roam.

We kind of ran out of dogs in our estate after the first few months.

People don't buy pets around here any more.

There's no point.

MISSING
Mr Tiddles
Contact: Mrs Capel

And the funny thing is that even though he's my big brother, *I'm* the one who has to mind *him*.

I mean, if I weren't there to help Dad, he'd get a lot hungrier than he does now.

Mum can't, you see. She has her work cut out keeping the smell inside the attic.

47

And like Dad always says, two pairs of hands are so much better than one.

Especially with cats.

Cats can be very wriggly.

THE END

There is absolutely no *way* I could sleep after that story.

I can still hear the clinking from the attic ...

The only way to stop the shivers is to hear another tale.

So who's next?

WWW.THENIGHTMARECLUB.COM